THIS WALKER BOOK BELONGS TO:

_____

_____

_____

_____

For Philippa, Richard,
Tim and Sophie

First published 1993
by Walker Books Ltd
87 Vauxhall Walk, London SE11 5HJ

This edition published 1994

12 14 15 13 11

© 1993 Jez Alborough

Printed in Hong Kong

British Library Cataloguing in Publication Data:
a catalogue record for this book is
available from the British Library

ISBN 0-7445-3607-3

CUDDLY DUDLEY

Jez Alborough

WALKER BOOKS
AND SUBSIDIARIES
LONDON • BOSTON • SYDNEY

Dudley loved to play.
He loved to play
jumping,

diving,

and splashing.
But most of all
Dudley loved to play ...

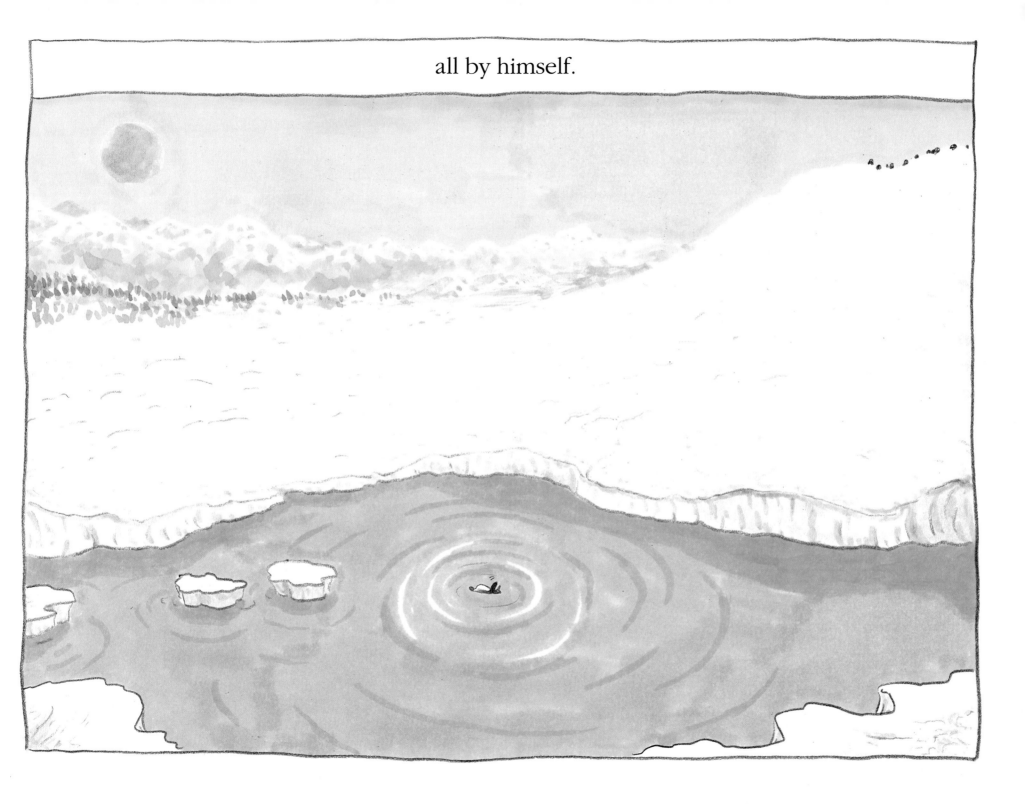

The trouble was, Dudley was such a lovely, cuddly penguin

that whenever his brothers and sisters found him on his own

they just couldn't resist having a huddle and a waddle and a cuddle with him.

"Go away," Dudley would say. "Leave me alone."

"We can't," came the reply. "You're just too cuddly, Dudley."

"I'm fed up with all your huddling and waddling and cuddling," said Dudley one day.

"I'm going to find a place where I can play all on my own." And off he went.

He waddled

and he toddled

for many, many miles

until,
quite by chance,

he found ...

a little wooden house which looked perfect for a penguin.

And it seemed to be empty.

"At last!" said Dudley. "A house of my own – a place where I can jump about all day without being disturbed."

Just then there came a rap-tap-tap at the little wooden door.

"It's us," said two of Dudley's sisters. "We followed your waddleprints. Can we come in?"

"No, you jolly well can't," said Dudley. "I'm very busy and I don't want to be disturbed, so please go away." And he shut the little wooden door and was alone once more.

"At last!" said Dudley. "A house of my own –

a place where I can splash about all day without being…"

Just then there came a rap-tap-tap at the little wooden door.

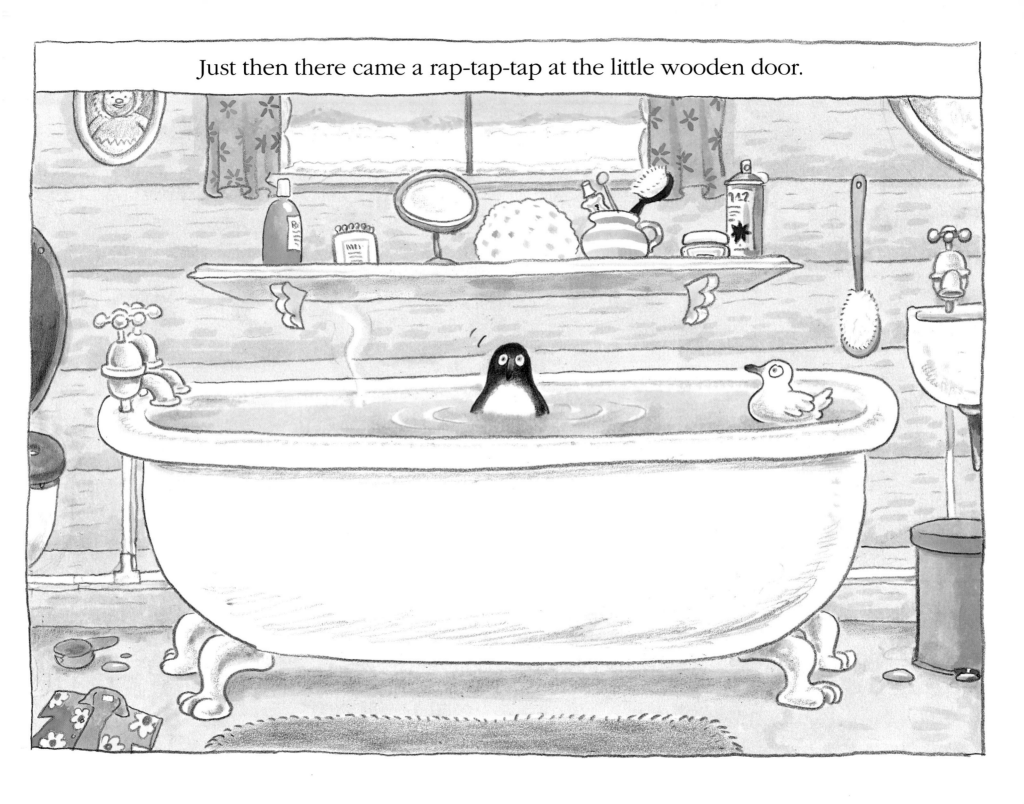

"It's us," said his brothers and sisters. "We followed your waddleprints.
Can we come in and…?"

"No, you jolly well can't," said Dudley. "I don't want to huddle and waddle and
cuddle. So for the very last time … STOP FOLLOWING ME AROUND!"
He slammed the little wooden door and was alone once more.

"At last!" sighed Dudley. "A house of my own…"

BANG, BANG, BANG went the little wooden door.

"That does it," he said. "When I catch those penguins I'll…"

But it wasn't the penguins at the little wooden door. It was a great big man. "My word!" said the great big man. "What an adorable penguin!"

"Give us a cuddle!" he cried, and chased Dudley all round the house and out into the snow.

Dudley ran

and ran

and escaped from the man.

Then he decided to head back home. But which way was home?

Crunch, crunch, crunch went Dudley, looking for some waddleprints to follow. But when night came, he was still alone … and completely lost … and now, for the first time, he was lonely. He climbed a hill to get a better view, and at the top he saw …

an enormous orange moon with hundreds of tiny sparkling stars huddled all around.

"Excuse me," said a penguin from the foot of the hill. "Have you finished being alone yet? Only we wondered, now that you're back … if you wouldn't mind … whether we could … it's just that you're so … *so…*"

"CUDDLY!" shouted Dudley.

And he bounced down the hill as fast as he could.

Then Dudley and all his brothers and sisters had the best huddling, waddling, cuddling session that they'd *ever* had. UNTIL …

MORE WALKER PAPERBACKS
For You to Enjoy
Also by Jez Alborough

WHERE'S MY TEDDY?

A small boy and a gigantic bear have a momentous encounter in the woods!

"A very appealing story … will bear endless repetition." *Patricia Hodge, The Mail on Sunday*

0-7445-3058-X   £4.99

IT'S THE BEAR!

They're back – little Eddy and the great big bear from the hilarious *Where's My Teddy?*
And this time the bear's not only huge, he's hungry too. No wonder Eddy is scared to picnic in the woods!

"One of the funniest picture books I've seen for a long time." *Books For Your Children*

0-7445-4385-1   £4.99

ICE-CREAM BEAR

Lazy bear just loves to dream of his favourite thing – ICE-CREAM!
But bear's sweet dream turns to sour nightmare, when he finds one day his cupboard's bare!

0-7445-6908-7   £4.99

HELLO, BEAKY

The intriguing and irresistible tale of a rain-forest bird's search for his identity.

"Lots of ecological detail." *The Times Educational Supplement*

0-7445-5486-1   £4.99

'Battle for Freedom'
An original concept by Amanda Brandon
© Amanda Brandon 2022

Illustrated by Bult Studios

Published by MAVERICK ARTS PUBLISHING LTD

Studio 11, City Business Centre, 6 Brighton Road,

Horsham, West Sussex, RH13 5BB

© Maverick Arts Publishing Limited May 2022

+44 (0)1403 256941

A CIP catalogue record for this book is available at the British Library.

ISBN 978-1-84886-883-0

www.maverickbooks.co.uk

This book is rated as: Brown Band (Guided Reading)

Battle for Freedom

Written by
Amanda Brandon

Illustrated by
Bult Studios

Chapter 1

Rowan shivered in the damp air and felt wet grass brush her legs. She tightened her leather belt and hurried across the muddy field. It would be a foggy night ahead.

She wanted to count the tribe's sheep before the mist came down and she could see no further.

As she approached the field, she saw the sheep had gathered together for warmth. Their woolly coats created a blanket in the barren field. She sighed with relief. At least she wouldn't have to round them up.

Suddenly, Rowan heard a laugh and the squelch of feet in the thick marsh mud. But they were not the feet of a four-legged sheep.

The noise was followed by a panicked bleat. Her heart thudded against her chest. She wasn't alone. Others were here too.

Rowan ducked behind a clump of bushes and peered over the top. Two Roman soldiers shouted as they struggled with a couple of sheep. The animals wriggled and kicked their hooves but the soldiers had tied them up tight.

Those were *her* sheep. Rowan scowled and clenched her fists. Without thinking, she charged out and yelled, "Stop!"

The soldiers looked startled. Then they laughed. They said something she couldn't understand and pointed at her.

All of Rowan's courage disappeared. What could she do against two Roman soldiers? She saw the glint of their swords. They had roped the animals together and their fists looked big and rough. She swallowed and felt her body freeze.

One soldier took a step nearer. Rowan feared he was going to grab her too. She jolted to life. All she could think to do was to *run!*

Chapter 2

Rowan sped off across the marshland. Thick mud oozed through her wooden sandals and briars ripped at her dress as she crashed blindly into a bush. She picked herself up and ran on.

She looked behind, fearful that the soldiers had followed. By now, the mist had thickened. It swirled in patches around her, making it hard to see ahead. Rowan panted and clutched her side as she stopped to catch her breath. When she calmed down, she listened. There was no sound. No bleats or shouts.

She stumbled on. Her legs were caked in mud and the ground underneath grew boggy. A splatter of rain trickled down her cheek. She needed to find shelter. If the Romans didn't catch her then she would be sucked under the treacherous marshes instead.

A patch of mist cleared and Rowan noticed the familiar shape of a shepherd's shelter a short way ahead. The small wooden hut was one she had often used when the wind lashed down and she had been too far from her village.

If she kept in a straight line, she would be able to reach it soon. She ran ahead, scowling at the thought of the Roman soldiers stealing her sheep. She remembered Queen Boudicca had told the tribe that the Romans wanted to take over. Perhaps she had been right.

"Before he died, my husband tried to protect us and made an arrangement with these Romans, but now they want to take everything," Boudicca had yelled. "Look! They whipped me for challenging them. We must stop them, once and for all."

The queen had waved her spear and showed the crowd her scars. Rowan admired her for standing up to the Romans. Boudicca had not let them bully her. Rowan wished she had been as brave when she had seen the soldiers in the sheep field.

Rowan remembered Boudicca's long red hair, the same colour as her own. Secretly, Rowan liked the idea of having hair fit for a queen. She had been named after the red rowan berries that grew near her village.

She often spent many hours washing and plaiting her hair, but she was too tired and hungry to think about it now.

She felt her stomach rumble as she staggered closer to the hut entrance. All she wanted to do was sleep. But as she entered, a hand grabbed her wrist.

Chapter 3

Rowan screamed and shook herself free. She staggered back.

"Help me!" a voice rasped.

She peered in the gloom to see a stranger, slumped at the back. His leg was twisted under him.

For a moment, she feared he was another Roman soldier but, when she looked again, she noticed he was wearing the simple woven clothes of an Iceni tribesman.

The stranger gazed at her with hope. His lips were dry and cracked and he looked tired and battered. Rowan guessed he must have been there some time. She strained to hear what he said.

"Attacked! Romans. They ambushed me," he gasped. "My leg hurts and I can't move." The stranger's shoulders slumped and his eyes closed.

Rowan crept closer and looked at his damaged leg. She had seen lambs slip and twist their new bones, and she knew how to fix them.

This man clearly needed her help. She murmured a few words of comfort and his eyes flickered.

Then, Rowan ripped some cloth from the bottom of her dress. She told him she would return with some water from a stream behind the hut to bathe his wounds.

She shivered as she left the shelter and picked her way carefully through the mud to the stream. She knelt and dipped the cloth in the water, all the while listening out for the soldiers. But there was no sound except the squelch of her own footsteps.

She hurried back to the hut to clean and bandage the man's wounds. The man flinched in pain as Rowan tended to him, but when she finished he gave a murmur of thanks. He closed his eyes and she saw him relax against the wall of the hut. Soon, he was breathing steadily and was fast asleep.

Rowan's eyes drooped. Soon she slept too. All thoughts of Romans slipped from her mind.

★★★

The next morning, Rowan gathered some berries for them to eat with the bread she already had with her. She found the juiciest and reddest berries to give to the stranger, who told her his name was Bran.

He grabbed them and tucked in. The juice oozed down his beard. "Ah! Thank you. I haven't eaten for a while. These are good."

"I'm sorry I screamed yesterday. I thought you were going to hurt me," Rowan said. "I was running from some Roman soldiers who were stealing my sheep."

"It looks like we both managed to escape those wretched invaders. Although I doubt I'll escape the queen's anger—I've failed in my mission. She has a fiery temper."

Her ears pricked up. "What mission?" Rowan asked.

"Boudicca sent me to keep watch on the Roman camp over the hill. I was to report back when I saw the soldiers pack up and let her know how many were there. Only, I'm not going to make it over to the camp with this leg of mine." He tapped the cloth bandage Rowan had tied.

"I'm good at counting," Rowan said proudly. "I count the sheep safely in each night. Well, at least that was what I was *meant* to do last night, until the Romans struck."

"Good at counting, eh?" Bran nodded approvingly. Rowan stood up straight. She tossed back her long hair and pulled her shoulders back.

Bran smiled but added, "Unfortunately, there's no way I'm able to get out of this hut to go counting soldiers." He sighed.

"Perhaps I could do it. My legs are strong enough to run to the field and count for you."

"Hmm. It could be dangerous. You said the soldiers were stealing sheep. You will need to stay out of sight of any Romans."

Rowan gulped. She hadn't thought of that. The memory of the soldier's huge fist and his sharp sword sprang to mind. Perhaps it wasn't such a good idea after all.

"Then again, you have an advantage. You are nimble and small. You could hide easily in the dips and trenches of the marshland without being seen." Bran stroked his beard.

Rowan thought hard. Her stomach flipped. Could she do it? She had looked after the sheep for most of her life and knew the marshes well. Maybe Bran was right. Yesterday's mist had lifted and this time she would be on her guard. Besides, anything that would help Boudicca stop the Romans was worth a try.

Bran said, "The legion has ten groups and each group has their own flag. I want you to tell me how many flags you can see. Then I will know how many soldiers there are. It will mean several trips to the field. Can you do it?"

"I can do it," she said firmly.

Chapter 4

Although the mist had cleared, the weather was still damp. Rowan hesitated at the front of the shelter. Perhaps she had been too hasty to suggest she return to spy on the soldiers.

She knew Bran had seen her check the horizon several times.

"Here!" He said. "I know a couple of tricks which might get you out of trouble." He showed her the best places to jab her elbows and stamp her feet so she could slip free if she was ever grabbed by a Roman soldier.

Rowan felt more confident and remembered the importance of the mission. She knew no one from her village would miss her as she was often away tending the sheep for days at a time. She set off with renewed hope. Taking care to stay out of sight, she made her way to the top of the field overlooking the Roman camp. She crept as close as she dared.

For the next couple of days, she returned to the sheep field to count the flags she could see and reported back to Bran. Eight... six... four... The numbers were going down.

He was delighted with her efforts. "This is just what I wanted to hear."

Rowan picked fruit from the trees nearby for them to eat and carried water in a small wooden bowl she found in the hut.

Slowly, the old Iceni soldier regained his strength.

Then one day, Rowan burst into the hut to say she had seen only a few soldiers at the site. The others were marching away in the distance.

Bran rubbed his hands. "This must mean the Romans are on the move. This is the moment Queen Boudicca is waiting for. She will see it as the ideal time to attack their capital, Camulodunum."

"Why has she waited so long?" Rowan asked as they sat by the small campfire she had lit to keep them warm at night. The wood crackled and she watched the sparks dance in the air when she poked a burning log. She warmed her cold hands and huddled closer to Bran.

"There have been rumours they are off to fight in another part of the country. Now, with most of the soldiers gone, this will be the ideal time to attack because the city will be left defenceless. It's vital I let the queen know." He stood up and stumbled towards the hut entrance, dragging his injured leg, but he grabbed the side and cried in pain.

Rowan gave a look of alarm and rushed to give him a long stick to lean on.

"Wretched leg! It's no use. I'll never make it across these fields to the queen's settlement." He pointed across the marshlands.

Although she had done a good job at bandaging his leg, Rowan saw he was not strong enough to make the journey. One stumble and he would be in the boggy marsh and she might never be able to pull him out.

"I'll go," she said. "I know these marshlands and creeks. You said it yourself, I'm small and nimble. I can find a safe path through."

Bran looked at her before he nodded. "You have proven yourself honest and able. Here, take my ring. Boudicca will recognise it. Tell her all that you have told me."

As soon as the morning sun rose, Rowan set off across the marshland. She was determined nothing would stop her.

Chapter 5

Rowan weaved her way through the boggy marshlands with ease. She made sure to avoid the thickest mud which oozed up through the tufts of grass. Once she was through the fields and on the hill, she could see the settlement not far away.

There was a large number of round huts set out and a curl of wood smoke drifted upwards from the nearest one she approached. Her heart beat fast. The queen's settlement was a lot bigger and noisier than her own village.

Rowan passed the hut with the fire and sniffed the inviting smell of cooking meat. She rubbed her empty stomach. The clang of iron rang out as two men chipped away, making tools nearby. They looked up, but Rowan ignored them and hurried towards the crowd which had gathered at the centre of the settlement. Their loud whoops and hollers filled the late afternoon air.

It was at the centre that Rowan saw Boudicca. She stood in her two-wheeled chariot. Her hair flew loose behind her in the wind and her fist pumped the air.

"We must fight these arrogant Romans. They call us savages and they want to take all our valuables. I say we shall never be their slaves."

"Hear! Hear!" the crowd yelled. "Freedom from the Romans."

"We must set aside our differences with other tribes and join forces so we can outnumber these Romans. Then we will take them by surprise." Boudicca said. "Who is with me?"

Again, the crowd echoed their approval and support.

Rowan wondered how she would ever get to the front of the people who jostled each other to get a good view. There were so many. She tried to duck and dive between their legs.

"Excuse me! Excuse me!" she said, but the crowd was too interested in seeing the queen. "Let me through! I've got an important message," she cried, but people ignored her. She squealed as a woman stood on her foot and she narrowly missed being cuffed on the side of the head by a man's large hands as he clapped with enthusiasm.

Eventually the queen stopped talking and took the reins. Her horses stamped the ground, impatient to leave. Rowan gulped. Surely Boudicca wasn't leaving the crowd. Not now. Rowan hadn't delivered her message!

I've failed, she thought and hot tears burned her cheeks. She had come so close.

Chapter 6

Rowan heard the clatter of hooves and the crowd parted to allow Boudicca's chariot through. She saw her chance.

She dived through the gap and threw herself in front of the chariot.

Dust rose up and the horses reared. They neighed and snorted. For a moment, Rowan thought she would be trampled. But Boudicca steadied the reins and Rowan dived to the side.

Unfortunately, she dived into the waiting arms of a guard, who yelled at her to stop. Rowan kicked and screamed but he held her firm.

Rowan remembered what Bran had told her. She let herself go limp and the guard relaxed his grip. Then she jabbed him with her elbows and stamped on his foot. The guard was taken by surprise and Rowan wriggled free.

She fell in the dust at Boudicca's feet and glanced up. The gold torc around the queen's neck glinted in the light and her eyes were fierce.

Rowan quickly picked herself up and dusted down her dress. "I have a message from Bran," she blurted out.

The guard tried to grab her again but Boudicca stopped him. "Wait! What is this message, girl?"

"The Romans are on the move. I've been counting them for the last few days as Bran told me to do. But he's injured. Look! I have his ring." Rowan held out the ring he had given her.

"She's just a common little thief," the guard spat and nursed his sore foot.

A small smile crossed Boudicca's face. "She certainly got the better of you," she said to him.

"Let's hear what she has to say. Tell me again."

The guard glared.

Rowan told the queen all that had happened. How the Romans had stolen her sheep and how she had found Bran injured in the shepherd's shelter. How each day the number of Roman flags she counted had decreased until finally, she spotted the soldiers on the march.

Boudicca clapped her hands. "This is the news I have been waiting for. Now our army can make our move. We will attack their precious Camulodunum and take these Romans by surprise."

The crowd, who had watched the scuffle with interest, whooped in support. "Let our rebellion begin," shouted a man and he thrust his spear in the air.

When the crowd drifted away, Rowan told Boudicca where to find Bran. The queen ordered some soldiers to help him home. Then she said to Rowan, "You certainly have courage, little one. You are a girl after my own heart. How would you like to join the start of our march to Camulodunum?"

Rowan beamed.

On the day the army set off on its long journey to the city, Rowan's face was painted a fearsome blue and she put a horn to her lips to blow a triumphant blast. Her heart filled with pride at the thought she had played her part in thwarting the Romans who had dared to take over her home.

Discussion Points

1. What did the Romans steal from Rowan?

2. Who did Rowan find inside the shepherd's shelter?
a) Boudicca
b) Bran
c) Romans

3. What was your favourite part of the story?

4. How did Rowan stop Boudicca from leaving so that she could deliver her message?

5. Why do you think it was a good sign that the number of Roman flags was going down?

6. Who was your favourite character and why?

7. There were moments in the story when Rowan had to be **brave**. Where do you think the story shows this most?

8. What do you think happens after the end of the story?

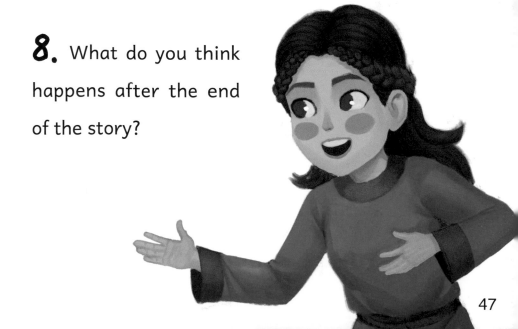

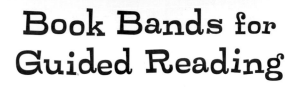

Book Bands for Guided Reading

The Institute of Education book banding system is a scale of colours that reflects the various levels of reading difficulty. The bands are assigned by taking into account the content, the language style, the layout and phonics. Word, phrase and sentence level work is also taken into consideration.

The Maverick Readers Scheme is a bright, attractive range of books covering the pink to grey bands. All of these books have been book banded for guided reading to the industry standard and edited by a leading educational consultant.

To view the whole Maverick Readers scheme, visit our website at

www.maverickearlyreaders.com

Or scan the QR code to view our scheme instantly!

Pink
Red
Yellow
Blue
Green
Orange
Turquoise
Purple
Gold
White
Lime
Brown
Grey

Maverick Chapter Readers
(From Lime to Grey Band)